Forever a Princess

The stories of Cinderella and Belle

retold by Sue Kassirer

Reader's Digest Children's Books™

Pleasantville, New York • Montréal, Québec • Bath, United Kingdom

Cinderella

A Dream Come True

✦ ✦➤✖✦➤✖✦➤✖✦➤✖✦➤✖✦➤✖✦➤✖✦ ✦

Every day was the same. I woke up early, cleaned the house, washed the dishes, mopped the floors, and took care of my Stepmother and two stepsisters.

But someday my dreams would come true. I just knew it. I would wear beautiful gowns and dance at fancy balls. Maybe I would even fall in love!

One day a messenger arrived with an invitation to a royal ball! I begged my Stepmother to let me go.

"I see no reason why you can't go," she said, "*if* you get all your work done."

As evening fell, I finished all my chores. But, just as I was about to leave for the ball, my stepsisters ruined the gown I was wearing. I ran into the garden and cried.

Suddenly, a Fairy Godmother appeared out of nowhere! She asked me why I was crying, and I told her.

With a wave of her wand, she turned my rags into a beautiful gown and sent me off to the ball in a glittering coach.

But she warned me, "On the twelfth stroke of midnight, the spell will be broken, and everything will be as it was before!"

The minute I walked into the ballroom, my eyes and the Prince's met. We danced…and danced…until the clock began to strike midnight.

In haste, I ran down the palace stairs and lost one of my glass slippers.

But it was that slipper that made the magic, for the Prince searched and searched for the one girl whose foot it would fit. And *I* was that girl!

We had a royal wedding. And we lived happily ever after. You see, my dream did come true. I fell in love with a wonderful Prince.

Belle

True Love

✦ ✦ ✕ ✦ ✦ ✕ ✦ ✦ ✕ ✦ ✦ ✕ ✦ ✦ ✕ ✦ ✦ ✕ ✦ ✦ ✕ ✦ ✦

As a child, I was not a princess. I was simply Belle, a dreamer and a reader. Books magically swept me away from the small, humdrum village in which I lived. And when I grew older, they saved me from Gaston—a handsome, but oh-so-boring suitor.

Then, one day, my life changed. I had to rescue Papa, who had been imprisoned by a cruel Beast in a castle. A spell had turned him into a Beast. I begged the Beast to take *me* instead of Papa, and although Papa protested, the Beast agreed and let him go.

There I was, the Beast's prisoner.
How mean he was—and how scary! But
then…he surprised me. He risked his life
to save me from a pack of vicious wolves.

Gradually, we became friends and I grew to enjoy his company. But still, I longed to see Papa. Out of kindness, the Beast let me go. I was free!

But guess what? I missed the Beast and discovered that I cared about him—especially when I heard that Gaston was planning to attack him! I leapt on my horse and got there just in time. I think the sight of me while he was on the rooftop gave the Beast the strength to fight off Gaston....

As the Beast lay there, badly wounded, I wept and said, "I love you," for that was how I felt.

Suddenly, the Beast turned into a most handsome prince! Looking into his eyes, I recognized the gentle and kind person I had learned to love.

All he needed to break the spell was to learn how to love and to be loved in return. After that, we married and lived happily ever after as prince and princess.

How to use this book

Now that you've met Cinderella and Belle, help them look glamorous as they prepare for the royal ball. They are depending on you to make them look dazzling.

- Carefully press out all purses and magnetic dresses for each princess.

- Now it's time to try some dresses on! The dolls and dresses are magnetic, so you just need to position them on the doll and they'll stay.

- Are you ready to make the dress even more dazzling? Use the jewels and stickers to make it look extra-special!

- Don't forget the accessory stickers! An elegant outfit is not complete without a pretty necklace, crown, or bouquet of flowers.

- To make your doll stand up, assemble the base as shown in figure on right.

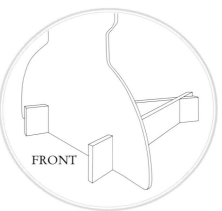

FRONT

- When you are finished playing, carefully remove the jewels and stickers from the doll and store them on the back cover of your book.